Title: Poor Boy, Rich Boy
Book Level: No
AR Points: Rating

S0-AYP-433

JER   J Easy Reading B   c.2
Bulla, Clyde Robert.
Poor boy, rich boy /

3 3774 00011 0958

DATE DUE

OCT 1 9 2010		
JAN 17 '12		
FEB 1 1 12		
AUG 0 8 2013		
SEP 1 8 2014		

Brodart Co.   Cat. # 55 137 001   Printed in USA

g

LIBRARY

OVE

BOOK

POOR BOY, RICH BOY

COVINA PUBLIC LIBRARY

An I CAN READ Book

Clyde Robert Bulla

POOR BOY, RICH BOY

J.
c. 2

ILLUSTRATIONS BY

Marcia Sewall

Harper & Row, Publishers

Poor Boy, Rich Boy
Text copyright © 1982 by Clyde Robert Bulla
Illustrations copyright © 1982 by Marcia Sewall
All rights reserved. No part of this book may be
used or reproduced in any manner whatsoever without
written permission except in the case of brief quotations
embodied in critical articles and reviews. Printed in
the United States of America. For information address
Harper & Row, Publishers, Inc., 10 East 53rd Street,
New York, N.Y. 10022. Published simultaneously in
Canada by Fitzhenry & Whiteside Limited, Toronto.

Library of Congress Cataloging in Publication Data
Bulla, Clyde Robert.
    Poor boy, rich boy.

    (An I can read book)
    SUMMARY: When a poor orphan is found by his rich
uncle, the boy's life changes dramatically.
    [1. Orphans—Fiction]   I. Sewall, Marcia.
II. Title.
PZ7.B912Pn 1982   [E]   79-2685
ISBN 0-06-020896-1
ISBN 0-06-020897-X (lib. bdg.)

First Edition

To Judy,
who showed me the horses

One day Coco was a poor boy.

The next day he was rich.

This is how it happened.

Just before the end of the war

a soldier found him

by the side of a road.

Coco was a baby then.

The soldier took him to the city.

"I can't take this child with me,"

he said. "What shall I do with him?"

A woman saw gold

on the child's finger.

"I'll take him," she said,

and the soldier left him with her.

The woman's name was Rosa.

She looked at the gold ring

on the child's finger.

There was a name on the ring.

"Coco," she said.

"So you are Coco."

She took the ring and sold it.

She bought food

for herself and the child.

She took Coco home.

Her house had been hit by bombs.

There was not much of it left.

But they had part of a room,

and they had food and a bed.

After the war,

Rosa went to work for a baker.

When Coco was old enough,

he worked, too.

He kept the shop clean.

He helped bake the bread.

Rosa said, "We must work hard,

because we are poor."

She said, "You may have

a mother and a father.

13

14

"Someday they may find you

and take you away.

So you see how it is.

I must not care too much for you.

You must not care too much for me."

One day a man came into the shop.

He said to Rosa,

"I was told you have a boy here.

I was told you are looking

for his mother and father."

"That is true," she said.

"I was told the boy had a ring

on his finger," said the man.

"Was there a name on the ring?"

"Yes," Rosa said.

"The name—" said the man.

"Was it Coco?"

"It was," she said.

"I gave him that ring!" said the man.
"Are you his father?" asked Rosa.

"His father and mother

died in the war," said the man.

"I am his Uncle Paul."

Rosa called Coco into the shop.

"This is your uncle," she said.

The man held Coco in his arms.

"Coco!" he said, over and over.

"I was all alone. Now I have you,

and you have me."

The man said to Rosa,

"You have kept my Coco for me.

How good you have been!"

"I must tell you this," she said.

"I sold his ring. We were hungry."

"You shall never be hungry again,"

said the man. "You shall have money—"

"I want nothing," said Rosa.

"You may take the boy and go."

The house had many rooms.

"Take any room you want,"

said Uncle Paul.

Coco found a little room

in the top of the house.

"I like this," he said.

"No, no," said Uncle Paul.

"This is a room for a servant.

It is not right for my Coco.

Here is the one you must have."

He showed Coco a big room.

It had thick rugs and a big bed.

Coco looked out the window.

He saw a road.

On the other side of the road were tree

"I want to give you everything,"

said Uncle Paul.

"What do you want, Coco? Tell me."

"I want to walk under the trees,"

said Coco.

"Yes, yes," said Uncle Paul.

"Someday you shall.

But tell me what you want."

"We had no trees in the city,"

said Coco. "That is what I want—

to walk under the trees."

Uncle Paul began to laugh.

"You don't understand," he said.

"You are rich now. You can have everything. What shall I give you?"

Coco did not answer.

"I know," said Uncle Paul.

"You need clothes. Come."

They went to the village

and bought clothes. They bought

boxes and boxes of clothes.

"Tell me what else you want,"

said Uncle Paul.

"Nothing else, thank you," said Coco.

They were on the street.

Coco looked into the shop windows.

In one of them he saw a seashell.

"Is it real?" he asked.

"Yes," said Uncle Paul.

"Would you like it?"

"No, thank you," said Coco.

"I was only looking at it,

because it is so big."

But the next day

he found the shell in his room.

His uncle had bought it for a surprise.

"Put it to your ear," said Uncle Paul.

"What do you hear?"

"I hear a roar," said Coco.

"That roar is like the sound

of the sea," said Uncle Paul.

"Have you ever been to the sea?"

"No," said Coco.

"Then I must take you there,"

said Uncle Paul.

In the morning

they went to the sea.

Coco liked the beach,

with the waves coming in.

He did not like the hotel

where they stayed.

It was too big,

and there were too many people.

But they soon left the hotel.

They drove along the sea
and stopped on a hill.

"Look down," said Uncle Paul.

Coco looked. He saw horses.

He had seen horses before.

He had seen them pull carts.

But he had never seen horses

such as these.

These horses were free.

They were playing on the beach.

They ran in and out of the water

with their manes and tails flying.

"They are so beautiful!" said Coco.

Uncle Paul told him,

"They are wild horses.

They live by the sea."

"Look!" said Coco.

"See the little horse.

It is the most beautiful of all."

The little horse was white as milk.

It played and splashed in the waves.

It ran along the sand.

Sometimes it ran

beside a big white horse

with a gray mane and tail.

"The big horse is its mother,"

said Coco.

"Don't you think so?"

"Yes, I think so," said Uncle Paul.

They sat on the hill for a long time.

Then people came to the beach,

and the horses ran away.

On the way home, Uncle Paul asked,

"Did you like your day by the sea?"

"Yes," said Coco.

"I liked the horses best."

The next day Coco slept till noon.

Uncle Paul came to wake him up.

"I've been away," he said. "I went

to see about a surprise for you."

"What is it?" asked Coco.

"You'll know tomorrow,"

said Uncle Paul.

"Now, what do you want to do today?"

Coco looked out the window.

He saw the trees across the road.

"I'd like to go over there," he said.

"Good," said Uncle Paul.

"We'll have a picnic."

But there was no time for a picnic.

People began to come to the house.

They were friends of Uncle Paul's.

They wanted to see Coco.

He sat up late.

Again he slept late in the morning.

Uncle Paul woke him up.

"Put on your clothes.

Quick!" he said. "Come with me."

They went past the stables.

They went to a pen

behind the stables.

Coco stood still.

There was a horse in the pen.

It was a white horse.

It was the little horse

they had seen on the beach.

"Some men caught him for me,"

said Uncle Paul.

"They just brought him in a truck.

Coco, are you surprised?"

Coco looked at the horse.

He looked at his uncle.

He said, "You hurt him!"

"What?" said Uncle Paul.

"There's blood on his neck," said Coco.

"The men had to put a rope on him,"

said Uncle Paul. "It left a mark.

That will soon be gone.

Coco, he is your horse."

"No!" said Coco.

"But—but you liked him the best," said Uncle Paul.

"I never said I wanted him," said Coco.

"You took him away from the sea. You took him away from his mother.

Now he is afraid. He is crying."

"Horses don't cry," said Uncle Paul.

"Yes, they do," said Coco.

"Can't you see?"

"You are a foolish boy,"

said Uncle Paul.

And Coco ran back to the house.

That night

Coco put a few clothes into a bag.

He had saved some bread from dinner.

He put that into the bag, too.

He put the bag under his arm

and went outside.

He went to the pen behind the stables.

The little horse was there.

He looked like a sad, white ghost.

Coco opened the gate.

Someone came up behind him.

Someone asked, "What are you doing?"

It was Uncle Paul.

He asked,

"Why did you open the gate?"

"So the little horse could go home,"
said Coco.

"He could not find his way home,"
said Uncle Paul.

He closed the gate.

He put his hand

on the bag under Coco's arm.

"What is this?"

"Some clothes and a piece of bread,"

said Coco.

"Were you going away?"

asked Uncle Paul.

"Yes," said Coco.

"To stay with Rosa, if she wants me."

"It's a long way," said Uncle Paul.

"Stay here tonight.

We can talk in the morning."

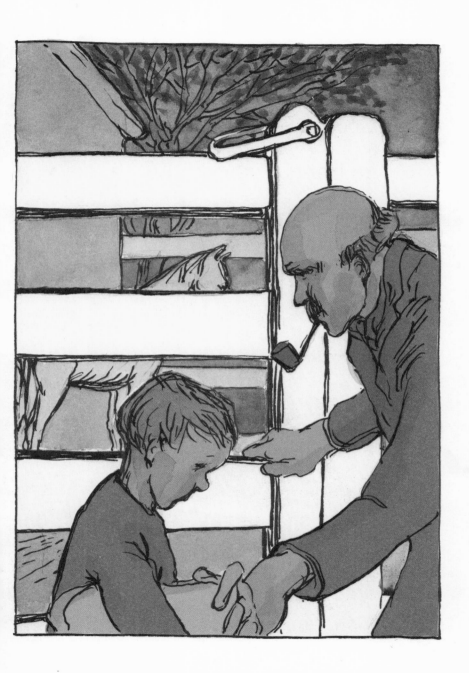

In the morning

Coco saw a truck

in front of the house.

"Come," said Uncle Paul.

"We are going to take

the little horse home."

They got into the car

and followed the truck down the road.

They followed it all the way

to the sea.

They went up on the hill and watched.

The truck stopped on the beach.

The horse was let out,

and the truck drove away.

The little horse was alone

on the beach.

He shook his head.

He took a few steps.

He ran into the sea and out.

Other horses came up

along the beach.

They made a circle around him.

One was the big white horse

with the gray mane and tail.

"The mother!" said Coco.

The horses began to run.

They kicked up sand and water.

They ran down the beach
until they were out of sight.
Coco and Uncle Paul went home.

"Do you want to go to Rosa's?"

asked Uncle Paul.

"She might not want me," said Coco.

"But *I* want you," said Uncle Paul.

He asked, "Would you like to walk

under the trees?"

"Yes," said Coco.

"Then go," said Uncle Paul.

Coco started and stopped.

He asked,

"Don't you want to come, too?"

"Do you want me?" asked Uncle Paul.

"Yes," said Coco.

They walked under the trees.

It was cool and quiet there.

The leaves moved a little,

and the sky showed through.

Coco began to feel happy.

He thought Uncle Paul was happy, too